The Captain Beard

by Laura J. Bobrow
illustrated by Jack Lindstrom

How **The Captain's Beard** Came to Be

When I was young my mother would send me to the grocery store on errands. As I walked along, I'd think, "What if . . . ? What if, when I turn the next corner . . . ?"

Before long I was off on an imaginary adventure. I would tell it to myself in mental pictures, not in words. The more pictures I saw, the more details I could imagine, the better the adventure.

Today I tell stories. I use words, but I still play "What if?", and I always imagine the pictures.

Sometimes I make up "What if?" for other people's stories. I change little things, add them, or take them away to see how the story might turn out. Recently I came across an old ballad, *Trade Winds*, by Wallace Irwin. In his ballad, a big wind blows things off a sailing ship. I found myself asking, "Hmm . . . what if 'trade winds' were to mean that things trade places?" The pictures I saw in my imagination made me laugh. I used Mr. Irwin's idea about the sailing ship, added my own variations, and the story, *The Captain's Beard*, was born.

This is a tall tale, a whopper, a lie. The fun in telling it, even though we know it is preposterous, is to pretend it's true. We're not fooling anyone. We're all laughing together at the same joke.

Try saying to yourself after you have read this story, "What if . . . ?"

—Laura J. Bobrow

P.S. Want to have a little more fun? When you're done reading *The Captain's Beard*, take a look at Mr. Irwin's ballad in the back of the book.

Let Me Tell You a Story

To my sister, Miriam Raphael, wordsmith

Published by Riverbank Press
801 94th Avenue North, St. Petersburg, Florida 33702

Copyright © 1995 by Riverbank Press,
a division of PAGES, Inc.

Printed in the United States of America

2 4 6 8 10 9 7 5 3 1

ISBN 0-87406-730-8

Jim Tarrington was just a young boy—not even into shaving—when he decided to become a sailor. He got himself a job on a brig, a two-masted sailing ship.

Jim was small for his age. The top of his head barely reached the bottom of the captain's beard.

Even so, the captain took a liking to Jim right away.

"You may be young and small for your age, Jim Tarrington," said the captain, "but it's plain to see that you are the finest sailor from here to Nebraska. I'm putting you in charge of all the other sailors."

"Aye-aye, sir!" said Jim.

Being in charge meant that
Jim got to wear a silver whistle and
give orders.

Jim told the sailors to heave anchor.

"Yo, heave ho!" they sang, and the ship
got under way.

Things went along pretty well—until the day the big wind blew.

Jim noticed that the captain looked worried.

The captain put his head up into the wind.

He sniffed at it.

He waggled his beard and sniffed again.

Then he wet his finger and let the wind blow on it.

"Jim, my lad, I hate to tell you this," said the captain, "but there's a BIG storm coming, with BIG winds. Mark my words, we're in for some BIG trouble! Haul down the mainsail! Take down the jib! And be quick about it!"

"Aye-aye, sir!"

Jim hopped to it.
He sent the sailors up
the masts to take care
of the sails.

But before they could get started,
the North wind began to blow.

And did it ever blow! It blew so strong, it blew so fierce, it blew the sailors right off the spars. Then it blew the spars off the masts.

Whoosh! It blasted everything clean off the deck.
It blew the pails and ropes away.
It blew the anchor away.
It even blew the nails right out of the planking!

Jim was amazed to see what happened next.

Out of the galley, apron flapping, flew the cook.

After the cook came all of his pots and pans and kettles and cans.

After them came the fire from the galley stove, and the coal from the galley bin.

Jim had never seen anything like it.

The captain turned his head to yell something to Jim, and the wind blew the beard right off the captain's face!

The words the captain said whizzed by Jim so fast
that he had to use a telescope to make them out.

"We're lost for sure, Jim Tarrington!" shouted the
captain. "Only one thing can save us now. We've got
half a chance if the wind turns around and blows back
from the South!"

Wellsirree, that's exactly what did happen.

The captain's words took to spinning in circles, just as if they were caught in the middle of a hurricane.

Then, before Jim could say "Jim Tarrington" twice, the wind began to blow straight back in from the South.

Back came the spars onto the masts.
Back came the sailors onto the spars.

That South wind blew so hard, it not only blew
back the nails, it hammered them back into the planking.

Back came the pails and the ropes onto the deck.
Back came the anchor.

And back came the cook. The wind blew him straight down into his galley.

After the cook came his pots and pans and kettles and cans. And not a drop of soup was spilled!

The fire blew back into the galley stove.

The coal blew back into the bin.

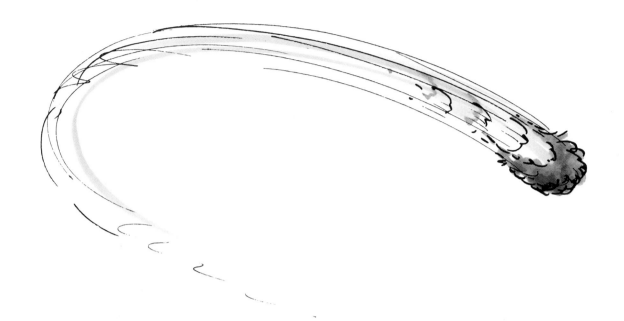

It was almost as if nothing had happened at all.

The only way anyone could tell that something really did happen was on account of what became of the captain's beard.

By the time the South wind blew the captain's beard back, Jim and the captain had traded places. The captain was standing where Jim had stood. Jim was standing where the captain had stood.

So the wind blew the captain's beard
back onto the wrong face!

The captain's beard didn't fit Jim Tarrington at first, but Jim was very proud of that beard.

He kept it,

and kept it,

and kept it . . .

. . . until finally he grew into it.

And as for the captain?
He had to go and grow another one.

About the Author

Professional storyteller, scholar, and researcher Laura J. Bobrow says she takes special delight in storytelling because it is the one discipline that encompasses each of her previous pursuits. She has achieved recognition as a sculptor, painter, poet, musician, lyricist, and author.

"There is visual excitement in storytelling," says Laura, "and there is rhythm and music, all together in the euphony of the spoken word."

Laura, whose audiocassettes have aired on National Public Radio, is on the Board of Directors of the Storytelling Center of New York. She is also on the Board of Directors of Nature in Legend and Story, which is devoted to understanding human relations with the natural world through literature.

She has conducted storytelling workshops at major universities and for the Annual Conference of the International Platform Association, of which she is a member. She also belongs to just about every storytelling group from New London, Connecticut, to Jonesborough, Tennessee.

Laura holds a degree in Education from Tufts University and pursues post-graduate studies in the humanities at S.U.N.Y. College at Purchase, New York. She grew up in Mount Vernon, New York, and has recently returned to occupy her childhood home.

This is her first book for Riverbank Press.

About the Illustrator

Jack Lindstrom was born in Minnesota. He has been an artist for many years. Mostly, he draws humorous pictures for books, newspapers, and periodicals. He also works with William Wells to produce a daily comic strip called "Executive Suite."

Jack, who graduated from the Minneapolis College of Art and Design, additionally operates an art studio in Minneapolis.

He is married to his high school sweetheart and has two grown children.